Rockets

CROOK CATCHERS

The Peanut
Prankster

Karen Wallace &
Judy Brown

Rockets

CROOK CATCHERS

Karen Wallace & Judy Brown

The Stuff-it-in Specials
The Minestrone Mob
The Sandwich Scam
The Peanut Prankster

First paperback edition 2000
First published 1999 in hardback by
A & C Black (Publishers) Ltd
35 Bedford Row, London WC1R 4JH

Text copyright © 1999 Karen Wallace
Illustrations copyright © 1999 Judy Brown

ISBN 0-7136-5127-X

A CIP catalogue record for this book is available
from the British Library.

Printed and bound by G. Z. Printek, Bilbao, Spain.

Chapter One

Lettuce Leef and Nimble Charlie were Crook Catchers to the Queen.

But today something most peculiar had happened. Splatter, the Queen's servant, had summoned them to an urgent meeting.

As they sat in the royal waiting room, a terrible noise ripped through the air. It sounded as if one of the royal corgis had swallowed a cat.

At that moment, Splatter raced
into the room.

He skidded on
the carpet...

...kicked over
a table...

...spilt a vase full
of flowers...

...and slipped
on the water.

He pulled himself up.
'It's the Queen,' he croaked.
'She looks terrible!'

Splatter's voice dropped to a whisper.

'You mean that terrible noise was the Queen?' gasped Nimble Charlie.

Splatter groaned. 'It's all El Bulgey Blabalotti's fault.'

Who's he?

Splatter shrugged. 'A fat man who sings terrible songs very loudly. He told her she had a wonderful voice.'

'What purple peanuts?' asked Lettuce Leef.
'The ones in purple boxes. She's hooked
on them,' muttered Splatter.
'El Bulgey Blabalotti said they were
good for her voice and now – '

Before he could say any more twenty royal corgis thundered into the room. It was a sure sign the Queen was on her way.

Chapter Two

'Splatter!' sang the Queen at the top of
her voice.

Splatter rolled his eyes and headed off.
'Right away, Your Majesty.'

Lettuce Leef knew it was rude to stare but she couldn't stop.
Nimble Charlie was so stunned he curtseyed by mistake.

The Queen was almost completely purple!

Her face was covered in purple blotches.

Her hair was
purple.

Her teeth
were purple!

She was even wearing a purple ball gown.
'Aren't we the greatest!' she bellowed,
twirling like a fairground ride.
'Now listen to our be-e-oo-utiful voice.'

And before Lettuce Leef or Nimble Charlie
could reply, the Queen started to sing.

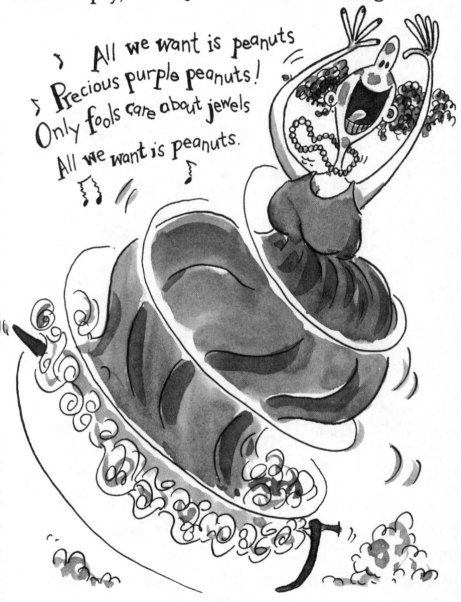

All we want is peanuts
Precious purple peanuts!
Only fools care about jewels
All we want is peanuts.

Lettuce Leef cleared her throat.
Nimble Charlie coughed.

'Told you I was good!' shouted the Queen.

Her eyes glittered. 'As for you two, tell
El Bulgey Blabalotti we will give him
all the royal jewels tomorrow.'

'Why? Why?' yelled the Queen.
'Then he will give us all the peanuts
we need!'

The Queen's purple face went purpler.
'Our voice is priceless, too,' she snarled.

At that moment Splatter appeared.
'Your peanuts, Your Majesty,' he muttered.

Nimble Charlie looked at Lettuce Leef.
Something had to be done fast.

'Excuse me, Your Majesty,' said Nimble
Charlie. 'Would you allow us to admire
your purple box a moment?'
'Go right ahead,' yodelled the Queen.

Just don't
touch the
peanuts!

Nimble Charlie carefully unwrapped the box. Lettuce Leef peered at the layers of purple tissue paper through her super-powerful magnifying glass.

Tucked inside a piece of purple paper was a single, long, shiny, purple hair.

'It's that fat singer's,' whispered Splatter.

'Stop whispering and gimme back my box!' bellowed the Queen.

Nimble Charlie patted Splatter on the shoulder. 'Don't worry,' he said.

Chapter Three

One hour later Lettuce Leef and Nimble Charlie stood in El Bulgey Blabalotti's front room.

There wasn't a single purple thing to be seen. Everything in the room was black or white.

What's more, there wasn't
a single purple hair to
be seen. El Bulgey
Blabalotti was
completely bald!
'So about these
purple peanuts,'
began Lettuce Leef.

'I no lika purple! I no lika peanuts!'
sang El Bulgey Blabalotti at the top
of his voice.

And hurry up with
your questions, I'm a
leaving the country
today.

'What about the Queen's singing lessons?'
said Nimble Charlie.
'Whatta Queen? Whatta lessons?'
bellowed El Bulgey Blabalotti.

'Then someone is pretending to be you,' said Lettuce Leef quietly.

El Bulgey Blabalotti puffed up like a huge bullfrog.

He opened his mouth and bellowed:

Nimble Charlie sat down. 'That's what we want to find out,' he said. He took the long, shiny, purple hair out of a plastic bag. 'Have you ever seen one of these before?' he asked.

'O solo mio!' howled El Bulgey Blabalotti.

'Who's Fatty Frederico?' asked
Lettuce Leef.

El Bulgey Blabalotti sank into a chair.
'A thief! A criminal! A fibber!' He began
to howl.

El Bulgey Blabalotti buried his head
in his arms.

Chapter Four

The next morning the Queen thumped
the piano in her music room and
bawled out her favourite song.

On the floor was an empty box of purple peanuts. Beside it was a full box of royal jewels!

Outside in the corridor Lettuce Leef and Nimble Charlie had an important meeting with Splatter.

The Palace doorbell rang. Splatter took a deep breath and went to answer it.

Lettuce Leef and Nimble Charlie hid behind a cupboard outside the music room.

At that moment a fat man with long
purple hair strode up the corridor.
Behind him Splatter carried an enormous
purple box.

They went into the music room and
slammed the door.

Chapter Five

'Did you bring me the peanuts?'
sang the Queen.

Fatty Frederico smiled a wide smile and
put the enormous purple box on the floor.

Outside, Lettuce Leef twisted the music
room doorhandle.

Nimble Charlie tapped on the cupboard.

El Bulgey Blabalotti stepped out of the
cupboard! Except he wasn't bald
any more. He had long purple hair
just like his brother.

All three of them walked into the room.
'I am El Bulgey Blabalotti,' cried
El Bulgey Blabalotti.

He glared at his brother.

'I know why you want these jewels,' cried El Bulgey.

'Silence!' thundered the Queen.
Her purple face began to go black.
Her purple fingers shook with rage.

Step forward the real El Bulgey Blabalotti!

Both men stepped forward.

From across the room Lettuce Leef
winked hard at Splatter.
It was the signal!

Splatter leapt forward and pulled two
lots of purple hair.

Chapter Six

Nimble Charlie was stunned.

Lettuce Leef was horrified.

Fatty Frederico was bald too!

Lettuce Leef looked at the Queen's face.
It was going blacker and blacker and
blacker.

Something had to be done fast!
She stared at El Bulgey.

A deep voice exploded like a huge velvet
firework and thundered
round the room.

'Sing!' ordered Lettuce Leef staring at
Fatty Frederico.
A strangled squawk like a turkey caught
in a mangle hung in the air.

The Queen picked up her purple handbag
and banged it over Fatty Frederico's head!

El Bulgey Blabalotti chased Fatty
Frederico from the room.

'Good riddance to bad rubbish,' shouted the Queen. Then she lifted up the skirt of her ball gown and kicked the box of purple peanuts out of the door.

Lettuce Leef and Nimble Charlie had never seen the Queen in such a temper before.

But Splatter had.

Don't worry, it's a good sign.

And sure enough a moment later the Queen started to laugh. She laughed until the tears poured down her face.

Silly us! Silly, silly us! The truth is we can't sing our way out of a paper bag!

The Queen threw herself down on a sofa.

Lettuce Leef bowed.

Nimble Charlie curtseyed by mistake.

'Splatter!' cried the Queen.
'How about a nice cup of tea?'
She winked and patted the cushions
beside her.

The End